D1384801

BAND GEEKS

Mr. Byrd
Flies the Nest

Calico

An Imprint of Magic Wagon
abdopublishing.com

by Amy Cobb
Illustrated by Anna Cattish

For Darius H. Skipworth, the brave.
And with sincerest gratitude to Mr. Vaught, who has
instilled a love of music in the hearts of many. —AC

abdopublishing.com

Published by Magic Wagon, a division of ABDO,
PO Box 398166, Minneapolis, Minnesota 55439.
Copyright © 2017 by Abdo Consulting Group, Inc.
International copyrights reserved in all countries. No part of this
book may be reproduced in any form without written permission from
the publisher. Calico™ is a trademark and logo of Magic Wagon.

Printed in the United States of America, North Mankato, Minnesota.
102016
012017

Written by Amy Cobb
Illustrated by Anna Cattish
Edited by Tamara L. Britton & Megan M. Gunderson
Designed by Christina Doffing
Art Directed by Candice Keimig

Publisher's Cataloging-in-Publication Data

Names: Cobb, Amy, author. | Cattish, Anna, illustrator.
Title: Mr. Byrd flies the nest / by Amy Cobb ; illustrated by Anna Cattish.
Description: Minneapolis, MN : Magic Wagon, 2017. | Series: Band geeks
Summary: The students in room 217 worry band director Mr. Byrd is
    leaving at the end of the year, so they plot to figure out the truth
    and find a way to make him stay.
Identifiers: LCCN 2016947367 | ISBN 9781624021732 (lib. bdg.) |
    ISBN 9781624022333 (ebook) | ISBN 9781624022630 (Read-to-me
    ebook)
Subjects: LCSH: Bands (Music)--Juvenile fiction. | Junior high
    schools--Juvenile fiction. | Middle schools--Juvenile fiction.
    Classification: DDC [Fic]--dc23
    LC record available at http:// /2016947367

TABLE OF CONTENTS

Chapter 1

NOT-SO-EARLY BYRD

Sherman Frye warmed up with jumping jacks. Baylor Meece and Yulia Glatt flicked clarinet reeds to see whose would go the farthest. And Zac Wiles flew paper airplanes all around room 217. It would have been hard to hear a real 747 jet over the roar of the noise in the Benton Bluff Junior High band room.

Basically, it was like any other day before class got started. But things would change as soon as Mr. Byrd, our band director, walked in. Everyone would scramble to their seats. The noise would cease immediately.

Mr. Byrd loved teaching us about music, but he took our lessons seriously. He was like a band room drill sergeant.

Where was Mr. Byrd, anyway? He was late. Again.

I wasn't the only one who noticed, either. Lemuel Soriano nudged me and said, "Hey, Miles. I wonder what's up with Mr. Byrd."

"He's been late nearly every day this week," I said.

Lem glanced at the clock, like he was sort of worried. "And Mr. Byrd is never late."

Lem should know. He was in eighth grade, so he'd been in Mr. Byrd's band room for a couple of years. Lem played trumpet, same as me. Except he was the best trumpet player in the band. That's why he sat in the first chair, next to me in second. But since I just moved up to the junior high band this year as a seventh grader, I was pretty happy with my spot.

And you never know. Next year when Lem went to high school, maybe his chair would be mine. Except I wouldn't exactly be sitting in Lem's actual chair. That's because of having muscular dystrophy. Since my legs didn't work so great, I sat in a wheelchair. Mr. Byrd could just move Lem's chair over to make room for mine.

Anyway, even though I was new to the band this year, I totally got what Lem was talking about. "You mean Mr. Byrd never *used* to be late," I said.

"Maybe he's printing sheet music, and there's a long wait in the copy room," Morgan Bryant said, whirling around. This was Morgan's first year in Byrd's band, too. She sat in the row in front of us with the other clarinet players.

Lem scrunched his nose, making his blue-framed glasses go lopsided. "But there wouldn't be a traffic jam at the copy machine every day."

"Yeah." I frowned. "Somehow, I don't think that's it."

"Okay, so where is he then?" Morgan asked.

I didn't answer Morgan because Mr. Byrd rushed into the band room then. He must've hurried because his face was red, like the sunset above the sandy beach on his shirt. Mr. Byrd always wore tropical shirts, usually paired with khaki shorts and flip-flops. It was spring now, but he'd dressed like that all winter, too.

"Sorry I'm running late, everyone!" Mr. Byrd said. "Get your instruments ready, and let's bop a concert B-flat scale."

And just like that, class began. We played up and down the scale a few times. Then we played some warm-up songs. After that, we practiced a new song for an upcoming end-of-year concert.

"Somebody was off," I whispered to Lem.

He nodded. "I heard it, too."

I waited for Mr. Byrd to nail 'em, like he always did. But today, he didn't seem to notice.

Instead, Byrd pulled out his phone. "Let's take a quick break, everyone," he said.

"Okay, something is seriously going on here," Lem said.

"Definitely," Morgan said. "Mr. Byrd just seems—"

"Distracted," I finished for Morgan. "That's it! Mr. Byrd is distracted."

"Distracted, *monsieur*?" Lem asked.

That was another thing about Lem. He randomly talked in French, but he only knew a few words. I asked Kori Neal about it once while we practiced a song together back in the fall. She said it started when Lem found out his ancestors were from France.

"Yeah," I went on. "It's like when I'm filming videos to post online, and my mom keeps asking what I want for dinner. She finally says, 'Miles Darr, you're distracted! For the ninety-ninth time, do you want spaghetti or meatloaf?'" I even put my hands on my hips to imitate her.

Lem and Morgan both laughed.

Then Morgan said, "Spaghetti!"

"*Oui!*" Lem agreed.

"That reminds me. I'm working on a new band video," I said. "When I upload it, check it out."

"*You're* distracted now," Morgan said. "We were talking about Mr. Byrd, and you started talking about uploading videos."

Morgan was right. Making videos sidetracked my brain. "Online presence is important. Bands get discovered that way all the time, and ours could be next," I said.

"Talent gets bands discovered," Morgan said. "Plus, hard work. If I directed our band, I'd make everyone practice extra hard." Morgan dreamed of being a famous conductor someday.

"But some music agent might see you in one of my videos," I said.

"Seriously, Miles?" she asked, like I was on to something.

I nodded. "Of course. The problem is, people have to develop their star quality, like me." I adjusted the newest hat in my collection and popped my suspenders. "My big break should arrive any second now."

"*Excusez-moi,*" Lem interrupted. "Now you're *both* distracted. Can we just talk about Byrd, here?"

"Sorry," Morgan and I said at the same time.

"*Merci,*" Lem said.

I'd been around Lem long enough to know that meant "thank you," so I said, "You're welcome."

But we couldn't talk about Mr. Byrd any more just then. Break time was over. Mr. Byrd stood on the podium, front and center again. For the second time today, he apologized. "Sorry, but I had to make an important phone call. Now where were we?" He shuffled through some papers. "Oh, yes. We were about to play 'Kangaroo Capers.' Don't let those eighth notes trip you up."

"What? 'Kangaroo Capers' doesn't have any eighth notes. He's thinking of some other song," Morgan said. She raised her hand, probably to tell Mr. Byrd. But he didn't seem to notice Morgan's hand waving in the air.

"One and two and ready and go!" Mr. Byrd clapped as he counted.

The song began with the woodwinds—the clarinets, flutes, and saxophones. Then the percussion joined in. Davis Beadle, Carmen Trochez, and the rest of the drummers played a steady beat. I licked my lips and buzzed into my trumpet as all of us in the brass section joined in with our parts, too.

After we played the last measure, I waited for Mr. Byrd to tell us to play the song one more time, like he usually did. Instead, he said, "Okay, that's a wrap. For the remainder of the class, please study your sheet music. Read every note and every rest in every measure. Finger along, don't actually play. Then come to class tomorrow prepared to play 'Kangaroo Capers' again. Any questions?"

"Yes, Morgan?" Mr. Byrd asked when Morgan raised her hand again.

"Would you like me to tutor anyone who might need some help? I don't mind," she said.

So then Zac made a big show of circling his fingers to form a halo and perching it above his head, which was hilarious.

But I knew Mr. Byrd wouldn't be happy about Zac goofing off in class. He got after Zac all the time for being a class clown. I counted down under my breath, "Three, two, one," waiting for Mr. Byrd to tell Zac to cut it out.

But Mr. Byrd didn't pay any attention to Zac today. All he said was, "Thank you for the generous offer, Morgan. But I have one more phone call to make, so I'd prefer to keep things quiet." Then he headed toward his desk.

I leaned over and whispered, "I told you, Lem. Byrd is definitely distracted."

Lem nodded. "*Oui.* I believe it."

"Something has his attention," Morgan chimed in, "but it's not us."

"So what is it?" Lem asked.

I thought for a second. "Or who is it?"

Then I got an idea. Baylor sat a couple of chairs down from Morgan. Besides playing clarinet, Baylor was a reporter for the school newspaper, the *Benton Bluff Bloodhound.* Everybody in the whole school knew if you wanted to know something, just ask Baylor.

After class, I wheeled my chair over to Baylor and said, "I think there's a breaking story in the band room." I wiggled my eyebrows up and down. "And Mr. Byrd's name is in the headline."

That grabbed Baylor's attention. "What's going on, Miles?"

"That's what we'd like to know, too," I said, nodding toward Lem and Morgan. "And we need your help."

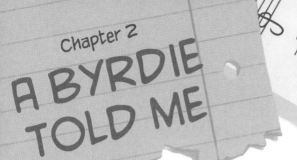

Chapter 2
A BYRDIE TOLD ME

"Let me get this straight," Baylor said to Lem, Morgan, and me the next day in the band room. "You think something is up with Mr. Byrd just because he was late for class yesterday?"

I shook my head. "Not just yesterday, but the day before that, too."

"*Oui*," Lem said. "And the day before that."

Baylor twirled her long, black braid. "You could be on to something here, but we don't want everybody else catching wind of it just yet. Let's go over there," she said, pointing toward the trophy case along one wall, "so we can talk in private."

"Good idea!" Morgan agreed.

When I wheeled myself over, Baylor began with, "I've been a school newspaper reporter for a few years now, so you can trust me. Everything you say is confidential. Got it?"

"Got it!" Lem, Morgan, and I said together.

"Okay, let me take some notes." Baylor whipped out a notebook and started scribbling away.

I unlocked my wheelchair brakes and moved in closer for a better look. So far, Baylor had written:

Subject: Mr. Elliot Byrd, Benton Bluff Junior High Band Director

Scene: Room 217

Sources: Morgan Bryant, Lem Soriano, Miles Darr

"You're good at this, Baylor," I said.

"Thanks!" She smiled. "But all I've written is the heading for my report."

"It looks official written down like that." I smiled, too. "Have you ever thought about uploading reporter videos? You could even get discovered—"

"Miles, enough with the videos! Focus!" Morgan said.

I hooked my thumbs in my suspenders. "Right. Sorry."

"No problem," Baylor said. "Now go ahead and give me your information."

We all began talking at once, and Baylor's pen flew across the page in her notebook. We mentioned how Mr. Byrd didn't flip out yesterday when someone's timing was way off. And how he took a break during class to take a phone call. And how he had mixed up the songs yesterday.

"He said there are eighth notes in 'Kangaroo Capers.' But there isn't a single eighth note in that song. And I know music. I mean, I have to," Morgan's voice went all dreamy then, "if I'm going to conduct an orchestra at Carnegie Hall." She stood a little straighter, as if she were already in negotiations with someone in New York City about this gig.

"And don't forget what happened with Zac," I said.

Just then a paper airplane came in for a crash landing right beside us.

Zac reached for it and said, "I heard my name."

"It's nothing, *monsieur*," Lem said quickly.

Zac didn't look like he bought that for a second. "You're not still talking about our last band potluck, are you? I didn't mean to make the whole percussion section sick, honest."

"No!" Baylor laughed. "This has nothing to do with your horrible fish casserole. Now scoot!" She motioned him on with her notebook.

"Maybe I don't want to scoot. At least not until I find out what's going on." Zac eyed Baylor's paper. "Are you writing an article on Byrd?"

"Shhhh!" We all shushed him.

Zac looked over his shoulder to make sure we were alone. Then he lowered his voice and asked, "What's the deal?"

"We're working on something, Zac." Baylor nodded toward us. "Lem, Miles, and Morgan are

my clients, and you're not. Now scoot!" she told him again.

Zac didn't budge. "For a second, I thought you guys were talking about Byrd acting strange lately."

"You mean, you noticed too?" I said.

Zac laughed. "Hey, just because I goof off a lot, doesn't mean I don't still notice stuff."

Boy, Zac was right about that. The goofing off part, at least. He was, like, the one person in band who never practiced. Or even played in class. Zac was forever forgetting his reeds, or his neck strap, or his entire saxophone. And that's what made it even weirder that Mr. Byrd didn't get on him for goofing off in class yesterday when he hung that pretend halo over his head.

"I have some information you might be interested in," Zac said, leaning in real close. He motioned for the rest of us to come closer, too.

So we did, waiting to hear what Zac had to say.

"Sorry," he whispered. "Since I'm not Baylor's client, my lips are zipped."

"He's faking!" Morgan groaned.

Zac stood up then and straightened the camouflage cap he always wore. "Hey, I'm not faking. But," he shrugged, "it's okay with me if you don't want to hear the details I've got." He started to walk away.

"Wait!" I figured Zac was bluffing. But then again, what if he wasn't? "Maybe we should let Zac in on this," I said.

"Are you kidding?" Morgan asked. "He'll probably mess up everything."

"What do you say, Lem?" I asked, glancing over at Zac.

Zac had a huge grin on his face and seemed pretty pleased that we were all gathered around talking about him right now.

While Lem thought about it, his lips twisted from side to side, like he was swishing some kind of yucky mouth rinse. "Maybe we should. But only if he has some real information," Lem said.

"Yeah, because if this is one of your dumb jokes, Zac Wiles," Morgan said, motioning toward the door, "you're outta here."

"Trust me. I've got information, all right," Zac said.

"So does everyone agree that Zac's in?" Baylor asked, her pen hovering below the Sources heading already written on her notebook page.

We all nodded, and Baylor wrote Zac's name right behind mine.

"Now," Morgan said, "spill it, Zac."

He motioned for everyone to move in closer, like he did earlier.

"You better be serious this time, Zac," I said.

"Yeah, no more jokes," Baylor said. "I added your name to my list, and I don't mind marking it off." She scribbled her pen in the air to demonstrate.

Zac made a cross over his camouflage jacket where his heart was. "I promise, this is for real." So when we were all huddled together, Zac whispered, "Mr. Byrd has a girlfriend."

Everybody was quiet. Then I finally said, "That's not funny, Zac."

Morgan rolled her eyes. "I knew including him was a mistake."

"I'm dead serious. Here's my best dead guy impersonation to prove it." Zac rolled his head sideways and stuck out his tongue. "See?"

"We get it, Zac!" Baylor elbowed him until he stopped.

Lem blinked. "Mr. Byrd has a girlfriend?"

"Snap out of it, Lem," I said, snapping my fingers. "I think you're going into some sort of shock."

Morgan still didn't look like she believed Zac. She even told him she didn't.

Zac shrugged. "Hey, it's the truth. It's like that Ripley's stuff. You can believe it, or not. But you'd better believe it," Zac went on, "because my cousin saw Mr. Byrd hanging out at the high school with Miss Fannin, the band director there."

Right now, I wasn't sure what I believed. If Mr. Byrd had a girlfriend, it would explain a lot, like why he suddenly seemed more forgetful. Last year, my grandma met this guy at the nursing home. When they started dating, Grandma acted all funny. She even forgot my birthday. Of course, maybe that didn't have as much to do with Grandma being in love as it did with her being eighty-three years old.

Mr. Byrd walked in then, and we had to wrap up our meeting. But before everyone headed toward their seats, Zac said, "See? Byrd's on his cell phone right now, and I bet it's her. My Girlfriend Theory is proven!"

Baylor hadn't said much. Since she was a reporter, I wondered what she thought, so I asked.

"We should have another meeting to see what else we can find out," Baylor said. "Are you in?"

"Definitely! Tomorrow's the weekend. How about then?" I said.

"For sure," Baylor agreed. So did everyone else.

The sooner we met, the better. And we'd put Zac's theory about Mr. Byrd having a girlfriend to the test.

Chapter 3

BYRD WATCH

"It looks like your friends are already here, Miles," Mom said the next morning when she dropped me off at Zac's house. Since my wheels didn't roll too well on grass, she pushed my wheelchair over to the picnic table in the backyard.

"Thanks, Mom," I said.

"Have fun, everyone!" Mom called as she left.

"*Au revoir, madame!*" Lem said.

Baylor and Morgan both waved good-bye.

I wasn't sure how much fun we'd have. Mom didn't know it, but this meeting was serious. We had to find out if Zac was right about Mr. Byrd being distracted lately because he had a girlfriend. Or if there was something else going on.

"Where is Zac?" I asked.

"It's Saturday. I bet he's sleeping in," Baylor said.

Morgan frowned. "Leave it to Zac to skip out on a meeting at his own house."

We all laughed at that one. And then Baylor pulled out her notebook to get started without him.

"Hang on!" I said. "What was that?" It was this strange growling sound.

Lem shrugged. "I don't know, but I heard it, too." He looked back over his shoulder.

"It came from over there." I pointed toward some shrubs by the garage.

"Mwah-ha-ha-ha!" Zac sprang from the bushes. "It was me! Man, you should've seen your faces." He died laughing.

Morgan didn't even crack a smile. "What were you doing?"

"Duh! Hiding from you. And you didn't see me because of my camouflage," Zac said, dusting off his clothes.

Zac wore pretty much camouflage everything. I tried talking him into wearing something, well, a little less green and brown, in some of the band videos I'd made. You know, to boost his style. But Zac insisted that camouflage *was* his style.

"Okay, Zac," Baylor said. "Please sit down and tell us about Mr. Byrd's girlfriend." She patted the wooden picnic table.

Zac sat beside Baylor. "Again? I already told you yesterday." But he retold his story anyway. "My cousin saw Byrd hanging out at the high school a couple of days ago with the band director, who is a girl. So Byrd's got a girlfriend. Simple."

Baylor flipped her notebook to a new page. "What did you say her name is?"

"It's Miss Fannin," Zac said.

Baylor jotted that down and asked, "So what does she look like? You know, short or tall? Hair color? Eye color?"

"I dunno." Zac shrugged. "My cousin didn't say."

I thought for a second and said, "I think I know how we can find out. Mr. Byrd lives right down the street from you. Right, Zac?"

"Yep." Zac nodded.

"Since we're all here, what if we just happen to go by Mr. Byrd's house? And maybe we'll just happen to see if he's at home by himself, or with Miss Fannin."

Baylor smiled. "An investigation. Great idea!"

"Let's go!" Lem said, hopping up from the table.

"Wait!" I grabbed Lem's arm. "Don't we need some kind of plan?"

So we decided that first we'd take the sidewalk past Mr. Byrd's house just to see if he was even home. No big thing, really.

"Hey, we need a name!" Zac said right before we got there.

"A name?" Baylor asked.

Zac nodded. "Yeah, it's like when the military has a mission. Sometimes they give it some cool name, like my dad served in Operation Desert Storm."

Now I got it. Since his dad was in the military, maybe that's why Zac liked wearing camouflage so much.

Morgan frowned. "Naming our mission is a silly idea."

"I think it's sort of cool," I said.

"Me too," Lem agreed.

Zac smiled at Morgan. "The majority wins."

"Whatever!" She shook her head.

Baylor flipped open her notebook again. "So what's a good name for our mission?"

"Maybe Mission on Spangler Street," Lem suggested.

"That isn't very fun," Morgan said.

"Or very original," I said, pointing at the street sign that Lem just got his idea from.

Lem shrugged. "Do you have something better?"

"We could choose a musical dynamic, like Mission: Mezzo Forte. That means medium loud," Morgan said, getting into choosing a name now. "Or Mission: Quintet. Five musicians performing together is a quintet, and there's five of us."

"Give it a rest, Morgan," Zac said.

When Morgan shot Zac a mean look, he said, "Hey, that was totally a joke. You were using band words, and I said 'rest,' like when there's silence for a beat of time in a measure. Get it?"

"Ha, good one," Morgan said, sarcastically.

"No offense," Lem said then, "but those names are no fun either."

I agreed with Lem. Morgan's ideas weren't so fun. But they sounded like something she'd come up with.

"Guys, choosing a name is taking too long," Baylor said.

She was right. Instead of getting information on Mr. Byrd, we were hanging around wasting time.

We were putting too much thought into choosing an operation name.

"I got it!" I finally said. "Let's choose something simple. Maybe something like Byrd Watch."

"Operation Byrd Watch," Baylor repeated.

Zac did a thumbs-up. "I like it!"

Lem and Morgan agreed, too, and Baylor wrote it down.

So we took off down the sidewalk again, heading toward Mr. Byrd's house. Just like that, Operation Byrd Watch was in action.

When we got closer, Zac held up one hand to stop us, like a traffic cop. "We can't walk right past Byrd's house all willy-nilly. It's like hunting. Or fishing. You have to be quiet. And move slow."

Zac seemed to know what he was talking about, so that's exactly what we did. Everybody took baby steps, and I eased my wheelchair forward along the pavement. We were closing in on Mr. Byrd's driveway when Baylor said, "Guys, check it out!"

"*Oui*," Lem said. "Mr. Byrd's yard is as tropical as the shirts he wears."

"No, not the pink flamingoes in his flower bed. Look!" Baylor pointed to a car parked at Mr. Byrd's house. "That could be a clue."

"Maybe it's Miss Fannin's car," I said.

"Right, I'll make a note. Red, two-door convertible," Baylor said, writing in her notebook.

"I can't picture Mr. Byrd riding around in that car," Morgan said.

"Me neither," Zac said. "The wind would blow that straw hat he wears right off his head."

We all laughed when Zac pretended to be Mr. Byrd, trying to hang on to his hat. He even took his own cap off and sailed it around, like it was flying through the air.

"But love makes people do weird stuff," I said, telling them about my grandma wearing lipstick when she got a boyfriend. "Every time she kisses me, she leaves wrinkly lip prints on my cheek."

"Eww!" Baylor said.

That got everybody laughing all over again. We didn't even notice Mr. Byrd standing outside now until he said, "What a surprise to see so many of my band kids!" He smiled. "I've been busier than usual lately, so I didn't forget about some extra practice scheduled this morning, did I?"

"Um, no. You didn't forget anything. Because we don't have practice today. It's Saturday, so we're just, you know, hanging out. And stuff." When Baylor got nervous, she talked super fast.

Then a car engine started up. Whoever drove that red convertible was leaving, but it was hard to see around Mr. Byrd. At least, not without looking like we were up to something suspicious. So the car pulled away before any of us got a good look at the driver. But it was definitely a lady.

"Nice car," Zac said.

"Isn't it?" Mr. Byrd said. "It's a classic. They just don't make cars like that anymore."

"Classics are special. And whoever was driving it must be pretty special, too, right?" Baylor asked, her reporter skills kicking in.

Mr. Byrd looked surprised for a second. Then he nodded. "Yes, very special. Now, if you're sure we don't have an extra practice scheduled today, I have errands to run and a ton of planning to do."

"Bye!" Morgan waved.

"See you on Monday!" Mr. Byrd said, swatting at a fly as he turned to go.

That's when I noticed the brochure in Mr. Byrd's hand. I wondered if the others saw it, too.

When we headed back toward Zac's house, I asked them. "Did anyone else check out Mr. Byrd's brochure?"

"What brochure?" Lem asked.

"The one he used to swat that fly buzzing around," I said.

"I didn't," Morgan said. "And I'm surprised you noticed it."

I shrugged. "Making videos means paying attention to small details. Anyway," I said, "the brochure was from a party tent rental place."

"So?" Zac asked.

"So," I said, "what if it's an engagement party? He even said he had a ton of planning to do."

Baylor flicked the button up and down on her pen while she thought about it. "Do you think they're that serious? I mean, wouldn't Mr. Byrd tell us something that big?"

"Wait a minute!" Zac said. "I just remembered, my cousin did say something about Miss Fannin getting married."

Suddenly, everything started adding up. Mr. Byrd was hanging out at the high school. He was late for class, and he was distracted when he was there. Plus, he stayed on his phone. A lot! Then yesterday, we found out Mr. Byrd had a girlfriend. Today, we found out that he was planning some kind of party.

Baylor and I looked at each other. It must've clicked in both of our brains at the same time.

"Are you thinking what I'm thinking?" Baylor asked.

"Yep," I said.

Then Baylor jotted down something in her notebook and held it up for everyone to see: Mr. Byrd is getting married!

"We solved the case!" I said, holding up my hand for high fives. "Operation Byrd Watch mission complete!"

Chapter 4
TWEET, TWEET

As soon as I wheeled into the band room on Monday, Baylor and Morgan came running over.

"Hey, Miles! I still can't believe we know Mr. Byrd's big secret!" Morgan said all singsongy.

Baylor smiled at me. "Isn't it exciting? Mr. Byrd found true love, and now he's getting married!" She and Morgan jumped up and down and did this high-pitched squeal.

I plugged my ears until their voices returned to a halfway normal tone that wouldn't shatter glass. Then I said, "Calm down, or the whole band will start asking questions."

Too late. Here came Hope James, Baylor's best friend. "What's going on?" Hope asked.

And Sherman was right behind Hope. He did jumping jacks all the way over to us. "Greetings, fellow bandmates! What's up?" he asked, sinking into some squats.

See, when most people think of warming up before band, they probably think of playing up and down some scales. Not Sherman. He told me once that it was just as important to prepare our bodies for playing music as it was our instruments. It all seemed sort of weird to me. But Sherman played flute and sat in the third chair, right behind Hope and Lilly Reyes. So who knows? Maybe Sherman was really onto something.

Anyway, Hope and Sherman just proved my point. Now even more of the band had gathered around, and they were all asking questions, too. "I told you so," I said to Baylor and Morgan.

"Maybe we should let them in on the big news," Morgan said.

Baylor didn't seem as sure. "I don't know. What do you think, Miles?"

I wasn't sure either. I looked over at Lem and Zac. "You guys should have a say in it, too."

"Let's tell 'em," Zac said.

And Lem agreed. "*Oui.*"

"Tell us what?" Hope asked.

Then Sherman started a chant. "Tell us! Tell us! Tell us!"

Baylor shushed everybody. "Miles, you should share the news since you're the one who started this whole thing off."

So I started with telling everybody how I was worried about Mr. Byrd being late for band practice. And about how when he was here, it was sort of like his mind was still somewhere else. "I mean, Mr. Byrd even lets Zac slide when he forgets his sheet music lately," I said.

"Hey, I'm not complaining about that." Zac grinned.

"Anyway," I went on, "Baylor, Morgan, Lem, Zac, and I did some investigating to see what's up with Mr. Byrd."

"And?" Sherman leaned in closer.

"And," I said, "Mr. Byrd is getting married!"

For a second, the whole band was super quiet, like we'd been transported from the band room to the school library. If we get busted for talking, Mrs. Appel, the librarian, bounces us right out of there. No kidding! She's brutal when it comes to library rules. "Quiet! This is a study space!"

But after everyone had time to think about it, the whole room exploded. *Kapow!* Then everybody started talking all at the same time.

"Are you serious?" Hope asked.

"As in du-du-du-dum?" Sherman began the wedding march.

"Of course, du-du-du-dum, you dumb dumb," Davis teased. "That's the song the marrying people walk down the aisle to right before they get married."

"Not the 'marrying people.' It's only the bride," Morgan corrected him.

"Oh. My. Gosh!" Baylor said. "What if instead of a pianist playing the wedding march, we play it?"

"You mean our band?" Morgan asked.

"Yes!" Baylor squealed.

I thought I might have to plug my ears again. But then Mr. Byrd walked in.

"Hey!" He clapped his hands. "Would someone please tell me what on earth is going on in here? I heard your voices from all the way down the hallway."

That library thing that happened earlier? Yeah. It happened all over again. Nobody said a word.

"Anyone?" Mr. Byrd said again.

Baylor looked at me, so I spoke up. "I think everyone is just extra happy today, sir."

Mr. Byrd definitely did not look happy. Right now, he looked crabbier than the crabs on the shirt he wore today. Its crabby eye stalks stared across the band room and focused on me.

"Extra happy, Miles? Well, I'm glad everyone is in a good mood, but this school year is far from over. In fact, we have a concert on our schedule in a few weeks. So," he folded his arms across his chest, "let me tell you what makes me extra happy.

That's students who are in their seats and ready to practice. Let's go!"

Mr. Byrd clapped his hands again, and we all grabbed our instruments and rushed to our seats. When everyone was settled, Mr. Byrd said, "Brass section, give me a concert G scale."

Brass section. That's me. I buzzed into my trumpet, up and down the scale, along with everyone else. When we finished, Mr. Byrd said, "Play it again, but trumpets only this time."

So I licked my lips and played the G scale again with the other trumpets. Mr. Byrd cupped his hand around one ear, listening intently. "Someone needs to work on their tone," Mr. Byrd said when we finished for the second time. "Any idea who that might be?"

I raised my hand. "I think it's me, sir."

Mr. Byrd nodded. "I think so, too, Miles. Try firming up the corners of your mouth, and you'll notice improvement." He even demonstrated by tightening the corners of his lips. "Work on that please, and thank you."

So Mr. Byrd moved on to working with the trombone section. He nailed Kori on her timing. Lem leaned over and whispered, "All of the wedding planning must be getting to *Monsieur* Byrd. He's always tough. But today, look out!"

Yeah, everybody knew Mr. Byrd was tough. Like with me just now. Think Mr. Byrd ever gave me special treatment just because I'm in a wheelchair? No way! He wanted me to be my best. And that's one of the things I liked best about him.

It was all because Mr. Byrd really loved music. And he loved teaching it, too. At least, he usually did. That's why I'd been sort of worried about him lately.

But now that I knew Mr. Byrd was busy with wedding plans and stuff, I got why he'd been distracted the last few weeks. He was probably super stressed, too.

"That's it!" I whispered back to Lem. "We should help Mr. Byrd."

"Help him? How?" Lem looked confused.

"Like today. When Mr. Byrd came in, everybody was out of their seats, and nobody had even put their instruments together yet. Right?"

Lem nodded.

"Maybe from now on, you and I should be in charge of making sure everyone is in their seats and ready to practice as soon as Mr. Byrd gets here. We could even play some scales to get warm-ups going. What do you think?"

"*Oui!* Great idea, Miles." Lem smiled.

I smiled, too. I could hardly wait to get started. Mr. Byrd would be super surprised tomorrow.

Chapter 5

TAKING FLIGHT

The next day, Lem and I didn't waste any time. We met each student as they came inside the band room.

"Grab your instrument," I said first.

Then Lem chimed in with, "And grab your seat."

When everyone had their instruments assembled, Lem and I went up by the podium. "In case you're wondering what's going on, we've decided to make Mr. Byrd's life easier," I began.

"It's the least we can do since Mr. Byrd is planning a wedding with his *fiancée*, which," Lem added, "is a French word, by the way."

"So for the rest of the year, we're done with goofing off. From now on, we need to be in our seats and ready to practice as soon as Mr. Byrd gets here," I explained.

"Let's warm up," Lem said.

Then I noticed Morgan waving her hand around. "Yes, Morgan?"

"Can I lead the warm-ups? I really could use the experience."

She was right. Leading a junior high band would probably look good on Morgan's résumé when she got to Carnegie Hall someday. I could even vouch for her.

"I'm cool with that," I said.

Morgan came up front with Lem and me. "One and two and ready and play," Morgan said, directing the band just like Mr. Byrd.

I was sort of surprised that everyone listened to us, but they did. "This is easier than I thought it would be, Lem," I said.

"*Oui, monsieur*," he said. "It's really working."

At least, it was until Zac came in.

When I told him to get his saxophone, he shook his head. "I can't. I've gotta talk to you guys and Baylor and Morgan. Now!" he said.

"Zac! Can't you see I'm directing the band here? And you're messing things up," Morgan complained.

"It's really important," Zac said. "I promise."

But whatever Zac had to tell us would have to wait.

"My goodness! Am I in the right band room?" Mr. Byrd joked as he walked in. He made a big show of looking all around the room. "It certainly looks familiar, and I think I recognize all of you. But this can't be room 217. My students are never in their seats with their instruments out ready to practice."

"We've already practiced some scales, too," Morgan said.

Mr. Byrd looked at Morgan, Lem, and me. "Thank you for your leadership today. And if you're after my job, Morgan, I'll certainly recommend you for the position. You'll be directing this band before you know it." He laughed like that was another joke.

Morgan smiled, and we all headed back to our seats.

"I told you he'd be surprised," I said, settling in next to Lem in the trumpet section.

"*Oui!*" Lem said. "And he was."

By then, Mr. Byrd stood on the podium. "Since you're all warmed up, let's get our kangaroo on."

Sherman must've liked that idea. He hopped up out of his seat and bounced in place. "Boing! Boing! Boing!" His brown curls looked like they'd spring right off his head.

"At ease there, Sherman. Save your energy for playing your flute," Mr. Byrd said, smiling. "Everyone, take out 'Kangaroo Capers.'" Then he looked at the saxophone section, where Zac sat with his hand up. "What is it, Zac?"

"I think I lost my sheet music," Zac said.

"Again?" Mr. Byrd sighed. "Go make yourself another copy." And when he handed the sheets to Zac, he joked, "Most kids fake being sick to hang out with the school nurse, but not our Zac. He prefers losing his sheet music, so he can hang out with Mr. Epley in the copy room."

Everyone laughed, and Zac said, "Hey, Mr. Epley is pretty cool."

"Hurry back, Zac," Mr. Byrd said, shaking his head. Then he clapped his hands and counted us into "Kangaroo Capers."

We were halfway through the song when Mr. Byrd said, "That's it! I like what I'm hearing, folks!"

The song ended with a big finish, and I could sort of picture kangaroos hopping around, like Sherman had earlier. The snappy tempo made it a fun song to play.

"What an improvement from last week," Mr. Byrd said. "Good things are happening in room 217. Let's keep it going. Please put up 'The Seashore Summer.'"

That was another song we were working on for the end-of-year concert. After we played it, Mr. Byrd said, "I really like that song, people. As you're playing, I can practically hear the ocean waves and feel the sand between my toes." He even struck a surfboard pose.

Lem leaned over and said, "Mr. Byrd is probably planning a honeymoon at the beach."

Lem was probably right. See, Mr. Byrd loved the beach, but he never took a vacation. Instead, Mr. Byrd went to band camp. And he held workshops every summer until school started up again. Since he didn't take real vacations, that was probably why he dressed like he was ready to hit the beach. But since he was getting married soon, of course he'd take a beach vacation this summer.

"I'm glad," I said back to Lem. "Mr. Byrd deserves some beach time."

"Oui!" Lem nodded.

"That's what music does, you know," Mr. Byrd went on. "Hearing a song carries you away to another time and place. It's sort of like what happens when you read a book, and the words carry you away. Except in music, you get swept away by the notes of a song."

Sherman laughed. "There aren't any music notes strong enough to sweep me away." He rolled up his sleeves to show off his muscles. "Check these out."

"Sherman, are you kidding? Your flute has bigger muscles than you," Zac said, walking back in from the copy room.

"Ha, ha," Sherman said in a sarcastic voice. But really, he was laughing.

"Sit down, Zac," Mr. Byrd said, looking like he was trying hard not to smile, too.

Things were back on track in the band room. Sherman and Zac had everyone cracking up. And we had Mr. Byrd back. He made learning music fun, just like he used to before he got distracted by wedding vows and wedding cakes.

I was starting to wonder why Mr. Byrd hadn't told us about the wedding yet, though. I mean, he even called us his "kids" sometimes. If we really were like some big band family, why wasn't Mr. Byrd sharing his major news with us?

"Now," Mr. Byrd said, "we're going to play 'The Seashore Summer' again. Only this time, I'm going to spend a few moments working with different sections. Sherman, since you have so much energy, we'll begin with the flutes."

That meant the rest of us had a short break while the flutes perfected their part of the song. I looked over some notes in the fourth measure that had been tripping me up. But then a paper airplane sailed right past my music stand.

When I looked up, Zac mouthed, "We need to talk." He stood by the trophy case, where we'd had our very first meeting a few days ago to talk about Mr. Byrd. And Baylor was with him.

I nudged Lem and tapped Morgan on the shoulder, and we headed over to the trophy case.

"What is it, Zac?" I asked.

"I've gotta tell you something," he said, looking real serious. I could tell Zac wasn't joking this time.

Morgan nodded. "Go on."

"It's about Mr. Byrd," Zac said. "My cousin told me that when Miss Fannin gets married, she's moving."

"Well, duh!" Morgan said. "That's what married couples do. You didn't think she'd still live at her house, and Mr. Byrd would live at his, did you?"

Baylor said, "Yeah, that isn't big news, Zac."

Zac shook his head. "You don't get it. Miss Fannin isn't moving into Mr. Byrd's house. She's moving to Florida."

Nobody said anything for a second. It was like our brains were trying to soak in the news but couldn't yet. That is until Baylor pulled out her notebook. She wrote: Mr. and Mrs. Elliot Byrd are moving to Florida.

"Now you've got it," Zac said.

I frowned. "But Mr. Byrd can't move away and leave us!"

Morgan's face looked red and blotchy, like she was about to cry. "He's my favorite teacher!"

"Are you sure he's moving, Zac?" Lem asked.

"Positive."

Everything made sense. Like when Mr. Byrd told Morgan earlier that she'd be directing the band before she knew it. And the way he'd talked about ocean waves and sand between his toes. I was happy for him then. But that was before I knew he was moving away forever to build sand castles.

"What should we do?" Lem asked.

"We have to stop Mr. Byrd," I said, "before he flies from our band room nest."

Chapter 6
EAGLE EYE

The only problem was that none of us were sure how to stop Mr. Byrd from moving away. But one thing we did know was that school would be out for summer break soon. That meant we didn't have a ton of time before the wedding. And before the just-married Mr. and Mrs. Byrd flew away to Florida, leaving us and the Benton Bluff Junior High band room far behind.

So after school that afternoon, Zac made plans for us all to meet his cousin at the high school. It was only a few miles away from our own school, and my mom drove Lem and me.

"Are you sure it's okay for you kids to hang out at the high school band room?" Mom asked, turning our van into the parking lot. A sign out front flashed

Welcome to Benton Bluff High School, Home of the Soaring Eagles. Just looking at it made me a little nervous. I hadn't thought about it much until now, but in a couple of years, this really would be my school. And since Lem was a grade ahead of me, he'd be a freshman here when school started back next fall.

"I'm positive it's cool, Mom," I finally said. "Zac's cousin goes to school here. She said a lot of the band kids hang out in the band room after school with Miss Fannin, the band director here."

"I suppose with Miss Fannin there to supervise, it will be fine. Besides, it's never too early to become acquainted with a new teacher," Mom said, looking back at me in her rearview mirror.

Mom had it partly right. Miss Fannin would be in the band room today. That's why Zac set this whole thing up, just so we could meet her. But since Miss Fannin was moving soon, she'd never be my band director.

Anyway, Mom unloaded my wheelchair and then and helped me into it. Morgan and Zac showed up with Baylor a few minutes later. So after we'd all agreed on a spot to meet our parents in a couple of hours, we headed down the sidewalk toward the main entrance.

"Where's your cousin meeting us, Zac?" I asked.

He shrugged. "I'm not sure. She said to text her when we got here."

"I hope she meets us soon," Lem said, tugging on the door. "Because we don't have the code to get in."

Luckily, one of the high schoolers hanging around punched in the code for us.

"*Merci, mademoiselle,*" Lem said.

At first, she looked surprised. Then she mumbled something that sounded like "weirdo." Lem must've heard it too because he huffed, "Nobody appreciates foreign languages these days."

But Lem forgot all about it once we were inside and got a text back from Zac's cousin. She gave us directions to the band room. We took the hall past the front office, then turned right past the cafeteria. After that, it was a straight shot to the band room at the end of the hall.

On our way there, Zac said, "I think we need a new mission name."

"Why?" Morgan asked. "Can't we just reinstate Operation Byrd Watch?"

Zac nodded. "Yeah, but that was the first phase of our mission. Now we're stepping things up."

"Zac's right," I said. "This is a real emergency."

Baylor pulled out her notebook. "I hope it doesn't take all day to pick out a new name, because we stunk at it the last time."

"*Oui!*" Lem laughed.

"Let's keep it simple again," I suggested. "What do you do when you want to keep a pet bird?" I asked.

"You mean like a parakeet or something?" Morgan asked.

I didn't have time to answer because Lem came up with something right away. "I'm good at riddles, and I've got this one," he said. "You put it in a cage."

I smiled. "Exactly!"

So as soon as Zac's cousin opened the door of Benton Bluff High's band room for us, Operation Caged Byrd began.

"Whoa! Check this place out!" Morgan said when we were inside. "It's huge."

"I'll probably get lost in here next year," Lem said.

"Bring a compass with you, and you'll be okay. But just in case, you should pack a survival kit," Zac joked.

"Make that three survival kits," Baylor said. "Don't forget, Zac and I will be here, too, Lem."

"I wish *I* could forget about it," I said.

Baylor looked at me then. "How come?"

I didn't say anything for a second. It was hitting me that not only were we losing Mr. Byrd when he moved to Florida, but Lem, Baylor, and Zac would all be leaving too. So maybe they wouldn't be moving thousands of miles away, like Mr. Byrd was. But since they were switching schools, they may as well be.

Baylor's great reporter skills kicked in, so she picked up on it. "Are you going to miss us next year when we're high schoolers, Miles?" she asked.

"Yeah," I said. "I really will."

She smiled. "Aw, we'll miss you, too. And you, Morgan."

"Thanks," Morgan said. "It is sort of sad."

Baylor leaned down to hug me, and she brought Morgan down with her. Lem joined in on it, too. When Zac just stood there, I motioned him in. "C'mon, Zac. Group hug here, and you're part of the group."

Zac looked like he didn't want to at first. But then he scanned the room to make sure nobody was looking, and he came in for a hug, too. After about two seconds, he said, "Hugging time's over." And he straightened his cap and pretended to smooth wrinkles from his camouflage jacket.

I figured Zac's cousin probably thought we were crazy. But when I looked around, she was gone. "Where'd your cousin go, Zac?"

"Over there. She had one rule about us coming today," he said. "Because we're still in junior high, we have to act like we don't know her."

"That's weird," Lem asked.

"Hey, high school kids are weird." Zac shrugged.

"No problem. We'll just stick to our plan," I said. "We don't want Mr. Byrd to leave. Now's our chance to convince Miss Fannin that moving to Florida is a terrible idea."

"We'll even beg if we have to." Zac folded his hands over like paws and panted like a dog.

"Attaboy," Baylor said, patting Zac's head. "Let's go, everyone."

As we made our way to the front of the band room, I thought about how lucky Morgan and I were. No matter what happened, Baylor, Lem, and

Zac wouldn't have Mr. Byrd for their band director next year anyway. But they knew how much we liked him, so they wanted to help us, and the whole rest of the band, too.

But when we got to Miss Fannin's desk, she wasn't there. Baylor went over to one of the other kids and asked, "Can you tell us where Miss Fannin is, please?"

"Sure, she took a box of stuff to her car. But if you use that door," he said, pointing, "you can probably catch her."

"Perfect!" Baylor said. "Thanks!"

The outside door led to a back parking lot, full of band trailers for hauling instruments and equipment to marching band shows. There were lots of other cars parked back there, too.

"We'll never find Miss Fannin. I mean, we don't even know what she looks like," Lem said.

"We don't know what she looks like," I said. "But we do know what her car looks like." I nodded toward a red convertible a few parking spaces down.

"Hey, it's the classic," Zac said.

Morgan frowned. "The classic?"

"Remember that day we saw her car at Mr. Byrd's house?" Zac said. "He called it a 'classic.'"

"I can't believe it!" Baylor said. She'd been leading the way, but now she stopped dead in her tracks and pointed. Good thing I can steer well, or I'd have rammed my wheelchair right into Baylor's heels.

I wondered what the big deal was, and then I knew. Miss Fannin was next to her car, but she wasn't alone. She was hugging some man. And he wasn't Mr. Byrd, either.

"Who is that guy?" Morgan asked.

"I don't know," Zac said. "But if she's two-timing Mr. Byrd, she's not as classy as her car."

When the guy hopped into his car and drove off, Lem looked ready to charge after him. "We've gotta tell Mr. Byrd that his fiancée is cheating on him," he said.

I knew how Lem felt. I was mad, too. But we had to think things through. "We can't just go and tell Mr. Byrd," I said. "We don't have any proof."

Baylor agreed. "True. If you go around saying stuff about people like that, it's called slander." She looked at me. "You'd make a great reporter."

"Thanks, but I think I'll stick with making videos for now," I said.

After a few minutes, Baylor said, "Miles, that's it! You should totally stick with making videos. But maybe Miss Fannin should star in your next one."

"Huh?" I said.

Baylor smiled when she said, "Don't worry. You'll get exactly what I'm talking about soon."

Yeah, I hoped so. Miss Fannin starring in my video? That was a crazy idea! I was pretty sure Baylor had completely lost it.

Chapter 7
LOVE BYRDS?

By Wednesday, I knew Baylor was totally bonkers for sure. And so was her idea. But since I'd gone along with Baylor's plan, I guess technically that made me bonkers, too.

"Tell me again why I agreed to come to Miss Fannin's house with you," I said to Baylor as we waited outside the brown brick house on Salyers Circle. The mailbox beside the door said C. Fannin in fancy gold lettering.

"Because Mr. Byrd is your favorite teacher. But he's getting married to Miss Fannin. And when they get married, they're moving to Florida. So it's bye-bye, Mr. Byrd. But he can't marry Miss Fannin because she's a cheater!" Baylor paused to take a breath. "Remember?"

"Like I could forget the Hugger," I said. That's what I'd nicknamed the not-Mr.-Byrd guy we saw hugging Miss Fannin in the high school parking lot a few days ago.

"Right." Baylor nodded. "And my plan will stop this wedding. Just trust me, okay?"

Baylor's plan was for us to interview Miss Fannin. She thought it would be helpful to spotlight a teacher at the high school each week for the *Benton Bluff Bloodhound*. That way the eighth graders would sort of get to know the new teachers they'd have in the fall.

Anyway, Baylor said we'd start out with talking to Miss Fannin about band. But then, we'd get the proof we needed that Miss Fannin was two-timing Mr. Byrd with the Hugger. And I'd get the whole thing on video, starring Miss Fannin.

"Okay," I finally said.

But this plan was risky. And Baylor was nervous about it, too. I could tell because she never stopped talking the whole time we headed to Miss Fannin's house.

I finally cut in to say, "Just slow down when you talk to Miss Fannin, so we don't look suspicious."

Baylor nodded and took a couple of slow, deep breaths. Then she rang Miss Fannin's doorbell.

Before swinging the door open, Miss Fannin nudged some moving boxes out of her way. She swiped her blonde hair from her forehead and said, "May I help you?"

Baylor introduced us both and asked Miss Fannin if she had time for an interview.

"I'm pretty busy." Miss Fannin looked hesitant at first. "But I suppose I can spare a few minutes."

"Great!" Baylor said when Miss Fannin waved us into her half-packed house. Then Baylor took her notebook from her backpack and nudged me to begin filming.

I aimed my phone camera at Miss Fannin and pressed the record button while Baylor fired off some questions. First, she asked Miss Fannin about her interest in music and why she decided to become a band director.

As Miss Fannin talked, I got why Mr. Byrd liked her. She smiled a lot. And she made me want to smile back. I almost wished Miss Fannin was going to be my band director when I moved up to high school. I probably would've liked her, too.

Then I remembered once when Mrs. Appel told us in the library not to judge a book by its cover. It was kind of the same way with Miss Fannin. On

the outside, she seemed nice. But on the inside, forget it! And if Mr. Byrd married Miss Fannin, his story wouldn't have a happy ending. The last chapter would be, like, "Mr. Byrd ended up alone and heartbroken. The end."

We couldn't let that happen. Not to Mr. Byrd. Baylor and I had to get the proof we needed about the Hugger before Byrd said "I do" to Miss Fannin.

"Miss Fannin, tell me what new students should expect in your band room next year," Baylor continued the interview.

"You know," Miss Fannin said, "I'm not sure if I'm the right person for this interview."

Baylor stopped taking notes. "How come?"

"Well, you might have heard by now that I won't be directing the high school band next year because I'm moving."

"That's too bad," Baylor said. The way she said it, I almost thought Baylor meant it. Maybe she couldn't stop herself from liking Miss Fannin, too.

"I'll miss my students." Miss Fannin looked really sad. "However, I look forward to seeing what the future has in store for me."

"Speaking of that, what do you see yourself doing in the future?" Baylor asked. She asked just the right questions to get the answers we needed.

Miss Fannin seemed to think about that one for a second. "I definitely see myself continuing to teach music to even more students once I get settled in Florida."

"Florida sounds nice," Baylor said.

"Yes," Miss Fannin smiled again now, "my fiancé loves the beach."

"I know," I couldn't keep from adding.

Miss Fannin frowned a little.

"What Miles means is, he knows because everybody loves the beach," Baylor said, keeping her cool.

"Miles," Miss Fannin said to me, "you look familiar. Have I seen you recently?"

Baylor didn't give me time to answer. She rushed right into her next question, "So when are you getting married?"

"In June." Miss Fannin blinked. "But I don't think that information is relevant to your band article."

"Have you set a date?" Baylor wasn't giving up.

And Miss Fannin wasn't giving in to Baylor's questions. "I remember you now. Both of you!" She looked from me to Baylor. "I saw you as I left Elliot's, er, Mr. Byrd's house a few weeks ago."

"Have you and Mr. Byrd set a wedding date yet?" Baylor pressed on.

Miss Fannin looked super surprised. Her mouth even dropped open a little. "Set a wedding date? With Mr. Byrd?" she asked.

Baylor nodded.

Miss Fannin laughed then. "I'm not marrying Mr. Byrd!"

Baylor and I looked at each other. Was Miss Fannin planning on leaving Mr. Byrd standing at the altar while she ran off with the Hugger? I'd seen it happen on TV weddings, but I'd never been to one like that in real life.

"I'm sorry," Miss Fannin said when she finally stopped laughing. "It's just, I can't believe you thought Mr. Byrd and I were getting married."

"So you're not getting married?" I asked.

"I am getting married, just not to Mr. Byrd." She pulled her phone from her pocket and showed us a picture. "This is Michael, my fiancé."

"Hey, that's the Hugger," I said. And I guess he really did like the beach, like Mr. Byrd, because he held a surfboard.

"The Hugger? Could you explain that, please?" Miss Fannin said.

We told Miss Fannin about seeing her in the school parking lot with the Hugger, only now we knew his real name was Michael. And we knew Miss Fannin wasn't cheating on Mr. Byrd, after all. So I gave myself permission to like her.

"I see what's happened here," Miss Fannin said. "You thought I was going to marry Mr. Byrd. And you were upset because you thought he was moving to Florida with me. Am I in the ballpark?"

"You just hit a home run over the fence and right out of the ballpark." I pretended to watch a baseball fly past the clouds.

Miss Fannin smiled. "I thought so. But Mr. Byrd is a dear friend. In fact, we graduated from college together. He was such a riot back then."

Now I wondered if we were talking about the same Mr. Byrd. Because *riot* wasn't a word I'd use to describe him. Tough, yes. Riot, no.

"It's been fun planning the upcoming retirement party with Mr. Byrd," Miss Fannin went on. "I look forward to getting the old gang back together next weekend."

After Miss Fannin returned from her trip down College Memory Lane, Baylor and I headed to the park across the street. While we waited for my mom to pick us up, Baylor talked nonstop about the retirement party Miss Fannin mentioned. "Did you pick up on that, Miles? I think there's something to it."

"We thought Mr. Byrd was getting married to Miss Fannin, too. And we wanted to prove she was two-timing Mr. Byrd with the Hugger. But instead," I patted my phone in my pocket, "we have thirty minutes of video that proves we were wrong about everything."

"Forget all that." Baylor waved her hand, like she was swatting away everything that had just happened. "I smell a new story here, Miles."

I sniffed the air. "That's funny, I don't smell anything."

"I'm serious!" Baylor said.

Baylor was always looking for the next big scoop. But this time, there was no story. She was way off about Mr. Byrd. And I knew it.

Chapter 8

LEAVING THE NEST

"Operation Caged Byrd was a giant flop," I said the next day after class in the band room. We were putting away our instruments when Baylor and I told Morgan, Lem, and Zac about the interview with Miss Fannin.

"Man!" Zac said. "Does that mean I've been bringing my sheet music and reeds to class for nothing?"

We all laughed. But it was true. Since we'd started trying to make Mr. Byrd's life easier when we thought he was planning a wedding, even Zac brought everything he needed to class.

"But there may be another story," Baylor began.

"Don't listen to her," I said. "There's no other story."

"Before the bell rings," Mr. Byrd interrupted then, "let's chat real quick, shall we?"

Everybody groaned. Mr. Byrd's "chats" were really lectures. And they were never quick. He leaned against his desk and said, "It's been brought to my attention that my personal life has been a hot topic of discussion lately."

Just great. I slumped in my wheelchair and hoped Mr. Byrd wasn't mad. Miss Fannin must've told him that Baylor and I stopped by her house to talk about their non-wedding. But Mr. Byrd didn't look upset. He was even holding back a smile.

"This has been one giant misunderstanding," he continued. "To clear things up, I currently have no marriage plans. I appreciate the concern, but my focus is entirely on music until I retire from this band room."

The bell rang then and Mr. Byrd called, "Don't forget to practice tonight! I expect you to nail that last measure in 'The Seashore Summer'!"

When we were all out in the hallway, Baylor said, "I told you so, Miles."

"You told Miles what?" Morgan asked.

"That there's a story here." Baylor pulled out her notebook and flipped it to a brand-new sheet. This time she wrote: Mr. Byrd is retiring!

"*Mais non!*" Lem said.

"But yes! Miss Fannin even admitted that she and Mr. Byrd have been planning a retirement party," Baylor said. "Didn't she, Miles?"

I nodded. "She did say that."

"But Mr. Byrd isn't that old," Morgan said.

"Maybe he's really eighty-nine, and he's discovered that cork grease is some kind of secret youth cream," Zac joked, pretending to slather some on. "No more wrinkles!"

Morgan laughed and said, "That's not it, Zac. His old high school band jacket hanging on the coat rack behind his desk says Class of '92. That doesn't make him old enough to retire."

She had a good point, but then Lem said, "*Au contraire, mon amie.* Sometimes people aren't that old when they retire. My aunt retired from one job and then took another one."

"That makes sense, I guess," Morgan said. "But what did you call me?"

Lem smiled. "*Mon amie.* It means 'my friend.'"

"Gotcha, *mon ami*," Morgan said.

Baylor sighed. "You guys can work on your French lesson later. Do you want Mr. Byrd to retire, or not?"

We all said, "Not!" at the same time.

Then I added, "But there's nothing we can do. I mean, he already has a retirement party planned and everything."

"We'll convince him to stay," Baylor said.

That sounded good. "But how do we do that?" I asked. Then I answered my own question. "I know! Old people like to feel young, sort of like I told you about my grandma wearing lipstick again."

"I refuse to put lipstick on Byrd," Zac cut in.

"No lipstick will be involved." I shook my head. "Mr. Byrd isn't technically old, right?"

"Right," Baylor agreed. "But he is getting there."

"Yeah, and he might be headed for one of those midlife crisis things I've heard people my mom's age talk about," I said. "So instead of a retirement party, what if we have a surprise party to make Mr. Byrd feel like a kid again?"

Morgan nodded. "I like it!"

"We can even decorate with stuff from the eighties," Baylor said, jotting down more notes.

"Don't forget the retro music!" Lem said.

He broke into the moonwalk, and I did the "Thriller" zombie moves with my arms.

"Nice, Miles!" Morgan said.

"Thanks!"

Baylor looked up from her notebook. "These ideas are great," she said. "But something else old people like is just feeling needed." Then she told us a story about her elderly neighbor knitting socks for newborn babies in the hospital.

"I didn't know Byrd was into knitting," Zac said.

"No, not knitting," Baylor said. "But what if Mr. Byrd thinks our band is so good that we don't need him anymore?"

Baylor was on to something. I mean, not to brag, but our band had improved a ton since the beginning of the school year. "Maybe Mr. Byrd thinks he's taught us all we need to know," I said.

"So how do we let him know we still need him?" Lem asked.

"That's easy," Zac said. "We just make a mess."

Baylor frowned. "Cut it out, Zac."

"Hey, I'm serious. It's like kindergarten art class. Back then, if we finger-painted the walls or squeezed glue on the reading circle rug, Mrs. Mohon called it a mess. And she cleaned it all up."

"I get it! Instead of making bad art, we'll make bad music," I said. "It'll be one big musical mess!"

Baylor was smiling now. "I love it!"

We all loved it. But we were hoping Mr. Byrd hated it. Then maybe he'd change his mind about retiring.

So for the next week, we planned our own surprise party for Mr. Byrd. The whole band got in on it. Baylor and Morgan planned the food. Baylor asked Hope to help Zac with the decorations. Lem was in charge of music, and Sherman volunteered to pitch in. And I worked on some new graphics to make a super cool party video.

Since the party was supposed to make Mr. Byrd feel young again, we called it Mission: Spring Chicken. But that was only part of our mission. The other part was to show Mr. Byrd how much we needed him in the band room. To do that, the band morphed into one giant musical mess.

By Thursday, Mr. Byrd caught on to us. "What is going on here, people?" he asked. "Our end-of-year concert is less than one month away." He took off the tropical straw hat he wore and fanned himself with it. "I've got to be honest with you, I'm not sure we'll be ready in time."

Baylor turned around and smiled at me. And I shot her a thumbs up. Our plan was working.

"Let's try 'The Seashore Summer' again from the top." Mr. Byrd put his hat back on and counted us into the song. "One and two and . . ."

Making a musical mess wasn't easy. I had to make myself do the opposite of everything Mr. Byrd had taught me. Instead of firming the corners of my mouth for a tight embouchure, I kept my lips loose. I moved my shoulders when I breathed instead of letting it come from my diaphragm. And my posture? It was lousy. My trumpet's bell pointed toward the floor, not straight out in front of me, like it was supposed to. Basically, I sounded terrible. The whole band did!

"Cut! Cut! Cut!" Mr. Byrd made a slashing motion. "What's the deal, guys? Good, no, great things were happening in room 217 last week. Now, your scales are scattered. Your perfect pitches are falling flat. And your measures are all mixed up." He stepped down from the podium. "Does anyone have any suggestions on how to fix this?"

I raised my hand.

"Yes, Miles?"

"I think we need more help from you, like maybe some one-on-one instruction," I said.

"I'm certainly open to more individual student lessons," Mr. Byrd said. "I'll create a spreadsheet with times and dates I'm available, and everyone can sign up." He pointed toward the ceiling. "We can only go up from here!"

Baylor raised her hand, too.

"Baylor?" Mr. Byrd said.

"When can we get started?" she asked.

"Ideally, the sooner, the better," Mr. Byrd said. "Any day will work nicely with my schedule, except this Saturday. I already have plans."

We all knew what Mr. Byrd's plans were— his retirement party. Saturday was only two days away. Our eighties surprise party for Mr. Byrd had to be so great, that he canceled his retirement party plans.

Chapter 9

SPRING CHICKEN

Before class was over yesterday, Lem suggested that we lead the next day's class. Mr. Byrd said he was willing to give almost anything a try at this point. So it worked out perfect for us to carry out our Mission: Spring Chicken party on Friday.

Baylor stopped Mr. Byrd before he could come into the band room. "Wait out here," she told him. "And no peeking either!"

"Yes, ma'am," Mr. Byrd said, saluting.

So we all rushed around the band room setting up everything.

"Snacks can go here," Morgan said, arranging chips and cookies on a table near the front of the room.

Hope hung up a sign that read Mr. Byrd's 1980s Party in bright neon colors. Then she and Zac went around hanging up some cassette tapes they'd made from cardboard. They'd even cut strips of brown tissue paper to make it look like the tape was unwound from the cassettes. Plus, they'd printed off pictures of some of those "big hair" bands and taped them all around the room.

"People in the eighties were weird," Davis said.

"I think they were kind of cool," Sherman said.

Davis smiled. "You'd fit right in, Sherman."

"Thank you," Sherman said, slipping on some black sunglasses. He'd even dressed up for the party. He wore a blue T-shirt under a white sports jacket with the sleeves rolled up to his elbows.

Sherman wasn't the only one who went all-out eighties. Carmen and Yulia wore leg warmers and styled their hair like the guys in the hair-band rock posters. Other girls wore hair scrunchies around their ponytails and long, dangly earrings.

"Hey, that reminds me!" Zac said. "I borrowed this from my dad." He plopped a blond wig on his head. It was shorter in the front and longer in the back.

"Whoa! What kind of hairstyle is that?" Davis asked.

"It's called a mullet. Dad said all the guys back then wore haircuts like this," Zac said. "I brought these, too. Catch!" He tossed some workout headbands to everyone who had their hands up.

I caught one, and slid it over my head. "Like, do I look, like, gnarly?" I asked, trying out some eighties slang I'd read on one of Hope's posters. It was covered in eighties phrases, like "Gag me with a spoon!" and "Radical!"

"Dude! You're, like, totally bad-o-rama!" Lem said.

We both started laughing.

"We're ready to bring Mr. Byrd in now," Hope said, taping one last poster up on the wall. It was a picture of a video game called Pac-Man with some red and blue ghost-looking things in a maze.

"I'll go get him," Baylor said. She made Mr. Byrd keep his eyes closed until they reached his desk, where we had a special surprise waiting for him. "Open!"

We all gathered around and when Mr. Byrd opened his eyes, he said, "What in the world?"

"It's you, Mr. Byrd!" Sherman said.

"Yes, I see that it's me," he said, picking up the photo we had enlarged. "But where did you find this picture of me in my old high school band uniform?"

Morgan smiled. "It was easy. My mom is in this Benton Bluff online history group. There were tons of old school pictures on the site, so we clicked through them all until we found one of you."

"*Oui*. Then we just made it bigger," Lem said.

Mr. Byrd studied the picture. "I remember the day this was taken," he finally said. "Our marching band had gone undefeated that year, and this was right before we marched onto the field at the state competition."

"It brings back good memories, huh?" I asked.

"Yes, Miles." Mr. Byrd nodded. "It sure does."

I glanced over at Baylor, and she gave me a thumbs-up. That's what this whole party was about, making Mr. Byrd feel young again. Then maybe he'd see he still had a lot of years left to teach, instead of going through with his retirement party tomorrow.

"Thank you all for being so thoughtful," Mr. Byrd said, placing the photo back on his desk. Then he looked around and said, "What is all of this?"

"Welcome to your 1980s party, Mr. Byrd," I said in my best announcer voice.

"Wait a minute." Mr. Byrd folded his arms across his chest. "We're having a tough week, so your idea of leading today's class is to throw a party?"

Uh-oh. He didn't like our party idea, after all. Mission: Spring Chicken could be grounded before it even took flight.

But then Lem explained, "We thought maybe we could use a break."

"And it's not just a regular party," Morgan said. "Miles and I planned eighties music games, too."

"We'll learn about that decade while we have some fun," I added.

"Fun and learning," Mr. Byrd said, uncrossing his arms. "I like it!"

So before Mr. Byrd could change his mind, I grabbed our eighties band matchup game and said, "Let's play!"

"How do you play?" Carmen asked.

"Basically, you just match the right picture to the right name of an eighties singer or band," Morgan explained.

Mr. Byrd said, "For example, I would just have to match a photo of Michael Jackson to his name?"

"You've got it!" I said. "But we didn't use his picture because that would've been way too easy."

"Definitely!" Baylor agreed. "Everybody knows the King of Pop."

We divided up into teams after that. The team with the most matches at the end of the game was the winner. Since Morgan and I had made the games, it wouldn't be fair for us to play. So we were the judges instead. Plus, it gave me the chance to tinker with my latest graphics to shoot some videos.

When Morgan held up the last photo, Mr. Byrd said, "That one's easy, too. Cyndi Lauper was one of my favorite artists. I still remember her hit song, 'Time After Time.'" He began humming it.

"We have a winner!" Morgan announced.

Then I wheeled over and handed Mr. Byrd and his team a picture we'd cut out of a trophy.

"Thank you, Miles," Mr. Byrd said, posing with the trophy and his team.

"Let me snap a picture," I said. "Smile, everyone!"

After that, Hope asked, "What are we playing next?"

"Next is eighties music trivia," I said.

Zac's hand shot up. "I want to be on Byrd's team!"

Of course, everybody did. And no wonder, because Mr. Byrd's team won that game, too.

"Our last game is called Name That Eighties Tune," Morgan announced.

"Look what I brought," I said, uncovering one more special surprise I'd hidden in the band room earlier.

"What is that?" Yulia asked.

"That," Mr. Byrd said, coming in for a closer look, "is what us 1980s kids called a boom box. Where'd you get this, Miles?"

"My uncle is the world's biggest pack rat. He had it in his garage," I said.

Mr. Byrd ran his hands over the speakers, which were as big as some dinner plates people ate off of. "It's a nice one. I used to take my old boom box everywhere."

"You must've had some muscles back then to lug that thing around," Sherman teased.

"Yeah," Baylor said. "It's as big as the suitcase I take to band camp."

"Carrying it around was no problem. You did it like this." Mr. Byrd picked up the boom box and hoisted it up on his shoulder. "See?"

"Hey, don't forget this!" Zac said, tossing his mullet wig to Mr. Byrd.

"You look, like, totally tubular, Mr. Byrd," Morgan said, borrowing one of the phrases from Hope's posters.

We listened to some eighties songs after that. And Mr. Byrd showed us some dance moves, like the robot and the electric slide. I bopped around in my chair and filmed all of the action. We were having a blast. That is, we were until Mr. Byrd's phone rang.

"Dial it down, guys!" he said, turning off the music and taking the phone call. A few seconds later, he said, "Yes, the party is at one o'clock. Please have the tents set up by eleven o'clock at the Benton Bluff Junior High football field."

"Oh, no!" Baylor said. "Even with this eighties party, Mr. Byrd's not changing his plans."

"Now what do we do?" Lem asked.

"Picture this. We'll swing in on ropes dangling from helicopters. Then we'll grab Mr. Byrd and whisk him away until he promises he won't retire," Zac suggested.

"No way," Morgan said. "I'm afraid of heights."

So while Mr. Byrd talked to the tent rental company, we brainstormed a few more ideas. I finally said, "What if we crash his party?"

"Seriously?" Zac asked.

"Sure," I said. "Why not? We know it's going

to be here at the football field at one o'clock tomorrow."

"I'm not busy then," Baylor said.

Morgan said, "Me neither."

So we had a new plan. Crashing Mr. Byrd's retirement bash was our last shot at keeping our favorite teacher in the band room. If that didn't work, we could always try Zac's idea and rent a helicopter.

Chapter 10
FLOCKING TOGETHER

The next day, we were near our school's football field just before one o'clock. That's when Mr. Byrd's retirement party was supposed to get started. Almost the whole band showed up to crash his bash. And we had a special surprise planned. If we couldn't convince Mr. Byrd to keep teaching us, we were at least going to give him the best going away present we could think of.

"Hold up!" I said to Lem, who led the way. "We can't just rush in. It's kind of like when we play our instruments. Our timing needs to be just right."

"Miles has a good point," Morgan said. "Let's see what's happening at the party first."

"Hey, I'll go with Miles to scout things out," Zac volunteered.

When everyone else in the band agreed, Zac and I headed toward the row of hedges that lined the side of the school closest to the football field. I had my phone ready to zoom in on Mr. Byrd's party so we could see what was going on.

"Something's wrong here," Zac said, as we settled in behind the bushes. "When you go hunting, you don't want to be seen. And look at you, Miles." He eyed me up and down. "That's a cool jacket, but you really stand out. Do you know what you need?"

"Camouflage?" I guessed.

Zac smiled. "Exactly!"

I wasn't so sure about that. I mean, I was really into fashionable clothes. My mom even teased me that I dressed better than she did. So camo didn't even exist in my closet.

Then Zac rummaged around in his backpack. "Good thing I brought this," he said. "Don't worry, man. I've got you covered."

Yeah, Zac seriously had me covered. Before I knew what was happening, he pulled this big camouflage thing from his backpack and plunked it right over me. It was like giant green and brown mosquito netting, with tiny holes all in it. And it completely covered me and my wheelchair.

"What is this anyway?" I asked.

"It's some leftover material from when I made my own hunting blind. You can see out, right?"

I nodded.

"But nobody can see you. You're camouflaged." Zac shot me a thumbs-up.

"That makes sense," I said. "In a truly weird sort of way."

We sat there for a few minutes after that, neither one of us saying anything. People were still showing up for Mr. Byrd's party. So while we waited for the right time to crash his bash, I decided to shoot some video footage to document the day.

"What are you doing?" Zac asked.

"Just shooting some scenes of the world from behind a hunting blind. I've never been hunting before."

"You should go sometime. It's fun."

"My sport is swimming," I said.

Zac looked sort of like he didn't believe me. I didn't blame him. I mean, if I were him, I probably wouldn't believe a kid in a wheelchair could swim either.

"I'm serious," I told him. "It's not like I'm some fast Olympic swimmer, or anything. But I have aquatic therapy a couple of times each week with my swim coach, Mr. Carloni." I patted the arms of my chair. "It's always nice to get into the pool and out of this thing."

"I bet," Zac said. "But do you want to know something funny?"

"If it's some dumb joke, not really," I said.

"Nah, it's no joke." Zac shook his head. "The funny thing is, I don't even notice your wheels."

I looked down at my wheelchair. It was black. And clunky. And it went everywhere I went. The wheels were sort of like having an extra set of legs. "I don't see how you couldn't notice it," I said.

"I guess it's because you wear the coolest hats and suspenders. And you're one awesome trumpet player, man. I bet you'll even get first chair next year with Lem in high school," Zac went on. "So instead of paying attention to your wheelchair, I just see you. Miles Darr."

Nobody had ever told me that before. Somehow, I thought this wheelchair sort of made me invisible sometimes. Maybe I was wrong. "Thanks, Zac!" I finally said. "I guess you're not a goof-off all of the time."

"Hey, do me a favor. Don't tell anybody." Zac laughed.

I laughed, too. "What happens in the hunting blind, stays in the hunting blind."

"You got it!"

"Ahem!" Footsteps thudded on the ground, and they were getting closer. "Is that you, Zac Wiles?"

"Uh-oh! It's Byrd!" Zac said.

It all happened so fast, Zac and I didn't have time to make a getaway.

"What is going on here?" Mr. Byrd asked. Then he started tugging on the hunting blind. "Miles, are you under there?"

"Yes, sir." I smiled at Byrd when he pulled the fabric up over my head.

Mr. Byrd looked from me to Zac. "Would you mind explaining what you're doing here?"

Zac said, "Sure, we can explain." But first, he yelled, "Hey, guys!" and motioned for the rest of the band to come on over.

Baylor headed our way, with Lem and Morgan right behind her and everyone else, too.

"You mean, the entire band is here?" Mr. Byrd asked. "And you even brought your instruments with you."

"Surprise!" I said.

Mr. Byrd looked confused. "This is a quite a surprise, but I still don't understand what's going on. Please explain. And start from the beginning."

So Baylor told Mr. Byrd about how Miss Fannin said she'd had fun planning the retirement party

with Mr. Byrd and how she looked forward to getting the old college gang back together again.

"Go on." Mr. Byrd nodded.

"And then," I said, "you told us you weren't getting married and that you were focused on music until you retired from the band room."

Zac said, "Hey, I'm no genius. But even I figured out you were throwing this party today to celebrate your secret retirement."

Sherman wiggled his eyebrows up and down. "We've been on to you for a while, Mr. Byrd."

"Yeah, we knew something was up when you started acting all distracted at band practice," Morgan said.

Mr. Byrd smiled. "I'm no genius either. But I think I just figured out why your playing has declined in the band room. You were playing badly on purpose, weren't you."

"We thought you were flying from our band room nest, Mr. Byrd," I said. "And we wanted you to see how much we need you to stick around to teach us."

"And the eighties party yesterday?" he said.

"We hoped you'd feel young again, *Monsieur* Byrd," Lem chimed in. "So you wouldn't want to retire."

Mr. Byrd nodded. "But there's one thing you've all forgotten."

"What's that?" Hope asked.

"Our band is like an extended family. I wouldn't keep anything that big from my band kids," Mr. Byrd said. "It's true that I have been distracted, and I apologize. Miss Fannin and I have been busy planning a retirement party, but it isn't for me."

Baylor frowned. "But if it's not for you—"

"The party is for our college band instructor, Dr. Sloane. He's been teaching for over forty years. And he's ready for a break."

"Don't say 'break,'" Sherman said. "I'm still sore from all of the break dancing we did yesterday."

Everyone laughed. And then Mr. Byrd said, "I do still have one question. Why do you all have your instrument cases?"

"It was a going-away surprise," Baylor said, holding up her clarinet.

"We've been working on 'The Summer Seashore' for our school concert, but we wanted to play it at your party. To show you how much you've taught us," I said.

Mr. Byrd glanced toward the party tent. "Could you still play it? For me and for everyone at the party?"

"Really?" Sherman asked.

"Really," Mr. Byrd said. "Assemble your instruments, and follow me."

So Mr. Byrd led us over to the tent and announced, "Ladies and gentleman, we're all gathered here to honor a wonderful band instructor and friend, Dr. Edmond Sloane. I can't think of a better way to show my gratitude for all that Dr. Sloane has taught me about music than to show him that his teaching continues on in my students." He pointed toward us. "I proudly present the Benton Bluff Junior High band."

On Mr. Byrd's count, we began to play "The Seashore Summer." We played our best for Dr. Sloane. And for Mr. Byrd. And for ourselves, too.

When we were finished, everyone clapped. Dr. Sloane and some other people even stood up.

Mr. Byrd said, "Take a bow, kids. I'm proud of you. And don't worry. I'm planning to teach music for a long time." He smiled. "I'll probably teach your kids and your grandkids. And who knows? Maybe even your great-grandkids."

"You'll be really old then, Mr. Byrd. You'll probably be in a wheelchair, like me," I said. "Maybe we can race."

"You're on, Miles."

"Nah, Miles, you won't be racing Mr. Byrd," Zac said.

"What do you mean?" I asked.

He grinned. "Some Hollywood agent will probably have already discovered you by then."

"Maybe." I smiled, too. "But maybe not."

Yeah, I always hoped someone would discover my videos online, and I'd be famous. But if it took a while, that was okay, too. Right now, I was sort of busy with my band.

Then I looked over and saw Baylor holding up the notebook she always kept with her. She'd written a new message: Mr. Byrd is staying in room 217!

And that was my favorite note so far.